Magic Ponies

Winter Wonderland

To Strawberry, pretty funster with attitude—SB

GROSSET & DUNLAP
Published by the Penguin Group
Penguin Group (USA) Inc., 375 Hudson Street, New York, New York 10014, USA

USA | Canada | UK | Ireland | Australia | New Zealand | India | South Africa | China
Penguin Books Ltd, Registered Offices: 80 Strand, London WC2R 0RL, England

For more information about the Penguin Group visit penguin.com

Text copyright © 2009 Sue Bentley. Illustrations copyright © 2009 Angela Swan. Cover illustration © 2009 Andrew Farley. First printed in Great Britain in 2009 by Penguin Books Ltd. First published in the United States in 2013 by Grosset & Dunlap, a division of Penguin Young Readers Group, 345 Hudson Street, New York, New York 10014. GROSSET & DUNLAP is a trademark of Penguin Group (USA) Inc. Printed in the U.S.A.

Library of Congress Cataloging-in-Publication Data is available.

ISBN 978-0-448-46786-3   10 9 8 7 6 5 4 3

Magic Ponies

Winter Wonderland

SUE BENTLEY

illustrated by Angela Swan

Grosset & Dunlap
An Imprint of Penguin Group (USA) Inc.

Prologue

Comet folded his gold-feathered
wings as he galloped across the hillside
on Rainbow Mist Island. The magic
pony felt a stir of hope. Surely his twin
sister had found her way home at last.

Destiny had been lost for so long.

Comet's cream-colored coat and
flowing gold mane and tail glistened in
the moonlight. Overhead, stars pricked

the midnight-blue sky. He sped onward, past distant mountaintops that were wreathed in the multicolored mist that gave Rainbow Mist Island its name.

Small stones struck deep-violet sparks from his shining hooves. The magic pony slowed as he caught a movement. *There—at the cave entrance in that steep rock face!*

Comet moved forward cautiously. He hoped it was another one of his Lightning Herd and not one of the dangerous dark horses. But he thought about how lonely he felt without his sister, and the magic pony decided to take a chance.

"Destiny?" he neighed softly.

An older horse with a wise expression stepped out from the cave.

"Your sister has not returned. But I am glad to see you again, my young friend," he said in a deep velvety whinny.

"Blaze!" Comet bowed his head before the leader of the Lightning Herd.

Blaze's dark eyes softened as he saw Comet's disappointment. He picked his way across the rocks until he stood next to the magic pony.

"I do not think Destiny will come back while she blames herself for losing our stone," Blaze neighed softly.

The Stone of Power protected the Lightning Herd from the dark horses who wanted to steal their magic. The stone had been lost when Comet and Destiny were cloud-racing. Comet had found the stone, but Destiny had already fled.

"I wish I could find her and tell her it

is safe to come home," Comet said sadly. "But I do not know where she is."

"The stone will help us!" Blaze struck the ground with one shining front hoof, and a fiery opal, glinting with many bright colors, appeared. "Come closer, Comet."

Comet's deep-violet eyes glowed with eagerness as he did as Blaze urged. The stone grew larger and brighter, and an image appeared in the rainbow depths. Comet saw Destiny galloping across a snow-covered field in a world far away.

He had to find her!

There was a bright flash of dazzling violet light, and a rainbow mist swirled around Comet. Where the magnificent golden-winged pony had been there now stood a sturdy mouse-colored Highland pony, with a darker gray mane and tail.

"Go now, Comet!" Blaze said urgently. "Use this disguise to find Destiny before the dark horses discover her!"

Comet's light-grayish-brown coat bloomed with violet sparks. He snorted softly as he felt the power building inside him. The rainbow mist swirled more thickly around him as it drew him in.

Chapter ONE

"Yay! I totally love snow!" Preeti Nimesh exclaimed.

She stood looking out of her bedroom window, where someone seemed to have thrown a big soft white blanket over the garden during the night. The whole world looked fresh and new.

Huge soft flakes, like cotton balls, were still falling. *Amazing*, she thought.

The snow's going to last forever!

Preeti ran out onto the landing. "Mom! Dad! Grandma! Have you looked out the window?" she called.

Her parents' bedroom door opened, and Mr. Nimesh came out in his pajamas, looking sleepy-eyed. "Do you know what time it is, Preeti? Where's the fire?" he asked, running a hand through his hair.

"There isn't one," Preeti said, grinning. "But I can't stay in bed anymore. Look!" She opened the curtains so her dad could peer outside.

A shifting curtain of snow blurred the white landscape of front lawns and the street beyond. Usually there would be cars and buses rushing past. But this morning, nothing was moving. Half-buried cars stood in many driveways.

"Look at that!" her dad exclaimed.
"The snow must be almost ten inches
deep. Your school's definitely going to be
closed, and I think I'll be walking to the
hospital."

Mr. Nimesh was a doctor. Luckily, his
hospital was only a few streets away. He

went back into the bedroom, and Preeti heard him talking to her mom.

"A snow day. Cool!" She clapped her hands in delight. She enjoyed all of her classes. But if it came to school or playing in the snow with her friends—it was no contest.

Another bedroom door opened and a small boy exploded into the hall. His dark hair was shiny, like Preeti's. But where hers was long and straight, his was short and curly.

"Snow! Snow! Snow! Have you seen it?" Viren cried, whirling around and waving his arms like a human windmill.

"Yeah! Of course I have!" Preeti said, rolling her eyes. "Didn't you just hear me and Dad talking about it?"

At six years old, Viren was three years

younger than his sister and small for his age. But he made up for it by having more energy than a box of frogs. He finally stopped spinning for long enough to make a face at her.

"I'm going to build a snow dinosaur in the garden!" he exclaimed, crossing his big brown eyes. "You can help me if you want."

"I'm not sure what I'm doing yet," Preeti replied. "I might call Lisa and Hayley, and ask them to come over."

"Lisa and Hayley are totally boring!" Viren sneered. "All they talk about is clothes and silly girly stuff on TV."

"No, they don't!" Preeti defended her two best friends. "You're just annoyed because they don't want to hang out with my extremely annoying little brother," she

said with slow emphasis.

"I don't want to hang out with them, either!" Viren stuck out his tongue, darted back into his bedroom, and slammed the door.

"Boys!" Preeti sighed as she went to get dressed in warm clothes and boots. Her grandma was making breakfast when Preeti came downstairs into the big eat-in kitchen. It was a big light room, with a table and chairs and comfy sofas set near patio doors that looked out onto the garden.

Sunetra Nimesh wore a pale green sari, and her graying dark hair was pinned into a neat bun at the back of her head. Small stud earrings twinkled at her ears. She looked up with a warm smile. "Good morning, darling."

"Hi, Grandma!" Preeti sang out, sitting at the table and helping herself to the delicious freshly made chapatis. She loved it when Grandma made these for a special treat. They were much tastier than their normal breakfast cereal.

Preeti was looking forward to the next few days. This was almost like having a winter vacation! As she ate, she began making plans. Maybe she'd dig the old sled out of the barn. Then she, Lisa, and Hayley could all go to the nearby park. There was a big hill there, and it would be fun to have races down the snow-covered slope.

She decided that she'd call them as soon as she finished breakfast.

"I wonder what the weather forecast is." Grandma switched on the TV.

Preeti looked up as the announcer began speaking.

"Heavy snow is expected for the next two weeks. People are advised not to travel unless it's absolutely necessary. Many roads are impassable, and most schools and many businesses are closed. There are no buses running at the moment . . ."

"Oh." Preeti's shoulders drooped. Hayley and Lisa both lived miles away, all the way across town. They weren't going to be able to get to her house. "It's not going to be much fun staying home from school if I'm all by myself," she said glumly.

"It is lucky that you and Viren can play with each other," Grandma said, pouring her a glass of milk.

Yeah, just great—not! Preeti thought. The last thing she felt like doing was babysitting her little brother.

"Good morning." Mrs. Nimesh greeted them both as she came in with Viren.

Preeti saw that her mom was wearing a sweat suit instead of the usual skirt and jacket she wore to the law firm. She guessed that she'd decided to work from home today.

Preeti excused herself and stood up. "I think I'll go to the barn and check on the pets. It's freezing outside, and they might need extra bedding."

"Aren't you glad that we haven't bought you that pony you wanted?" her mom commented. "Imagine having to muck out in this awful weather."

"I wouldn't mind," Preeti said at once. She meant it, too. She knew she'd do anything for a real pony of her own. She and Lisa and Hayley talked about them all the time.

"I'll help you!" Viren said, grabbing a

chapati and leaping up.

Grandma put a hand on his arm. "No, you will not. Stay there now. Eat," she urged. "Your sister can feed those rabbits and guinea pigs."

Preeti grabbed her coat from the mudroom and went outside. The air smelled cold and clean, with a chalky freshness. An icy wind was now blowing, and cold snowflakes stung her face and stuck to her eyelashes. She wondered if Lisa and Hayley were missing her as much as she was missing them.

Preeti pulled up her collar as she trudged through the deep snow. Her boots sank almost up to their tops as she picked her way slowly to the huge old barn at the edge of the garden. Beyond it was a blurred white view of open fields

and woods. Opening the barn door, she
went inside.

A warm smell of clean animals met
her. The far end of the barn housed
her dad's lawn mower, workbench, and
gardening stuff. Three large cages stood
against one wall.

"Hi, guys!" Preeti said, bending down
to talk to the bunnies and guinea pigs.

"Guess what. It's snowing outside! It's a good thing you're all cozy in here."

The little animals came snuffling up to the wire mesh to greet her. Her favorites were two handsome guinea pigs, called Chandra and Surya. Surya had golden fur that grew in swirly rosettes. And Chandra had petal-soft silver-tipped gray fur.

Preeti filled water bottles, tipped food into bowls, and replaced soiled bedding. Luckily she had recently stocked up on food. A friendly local farmer had sold them a huge bale of straw and a bunch of hay. So no matter how long the snow lasted, she knew that the animals would be warm and well fed.

She had just finished cleaning up when there was a bright flash of violet light and a shimmering cloud appeared

in the center of the barn. Preeti saw
twinkling crystal droplets forming on her
coat sleeves.

"Oh!" She narrowed her eyes as
she tried to see through the strange
multicolored mist. Had some kind of
weird ice storm blown into the barn?

As the mist began to fade, Preeti saw
that a pony was walking toward her. It was
sturdily built, with a well-shaped head,
a pretty light-grayish-brown coat, and a
darker gray mane and tail.

"Can you help me, please?" it asked in
a velvety neigh.

Chapter
TWO

Preeti felt her mouth drop open as she stared at the pretty pony in complete shock. She must have been so amazed at seeing it just appear in their barn that she was imagining things. There was no way a pony could talk!

"Where did you just come from? How did you get in here?" she murmured aloud to herself.

The pony flared its nostrils and lifted
its head. "I have just arrived here from far
away," it whinnied.

Preeti did a double take. "Y-y-you really
c-c-can talk? But . . . but how come?"

"All the other magical Lightning
Horses in my herd can talk," the pony told
her proudly. "My name is Comet. What is
yours?"

Preeti still couldn't believe this was
really happening. It was like something out
of a fairy tale. She felt like pinching herself
to make sure she wasn't dreaming.

"I—I'm . . . um, Preeti Nimesh," she
found herself saying. "I live here with my
parents, my grandma, and my little brother,
Viren."

Comet dipped his head in a formal bow,
and his dark gray mane swung forward.

"I am honored to meet you, Preeti."

"Er . . . me too," Preeti, said, wondering if she should curtsy or something. She settled for bowing her head in a jerky little movement. "Did you say that you came from far away? Like a different town or something?"

"A lot farther. I live in another world, on Rainbow Mist Island, with my twin sister, Destiny."

"Really? Cool! Is she outside in the snow?" Preeti asked, fascinated, about to go back into the garden and look for another talking pony.

Comet shook his head. "Destiny is here in your world, but she is in hiding. She fled here after the Stone of Power was lost during a game of cloud-racing. This stone protects our Lightning Herd from the dark horses who want to steal our magic. I found it, but Destiny had already run away. I have come to find her and take her home."

Preeti swallowed hard as she stared at the amazing pony, who, she noticed, had beautiful glowing deep-violet eyes. He looked like a Highland pony she had seen in one of her magazines.

Everything Comet had told her

sounded so strange and magical. She was still having trouble taking it all in. But one thing in particular fascinated her.

"You say you were cloud-racing? But how . . ."

Comet's large eyes widened. "Stand back, please," he snorted.

Preeti felt a warm tingling sensation flowing down to her fingertips as bright violet sparks bloomed in his mouse-colored coat, and more shimmering rainbow mist billowed around him. The sturdy Highland pony was gone, and in its place was a pale-cream pony with a long flowing mane and tail that sparkled like spun gold thread. But it was the spreading gold-feathered wings springing from his shoulders that took Preeti's breath away.

"Oh!" she gasped in wonderment as she gazed at the magnificent sight. She had never seen anything so beautiful in her entire life. "Comet?"

"Yes, it is still me, Preeti. Do not be alarmed," Comet said in a deep velvety neigh.

Before Preeti had time to get used to seeing Comet in his true form, there was another burst of violet sparkles, and the multicolored mist dissolved into shimmering dust, revealing the sturdy gray-brown pony once more.

"Wow! That's an amazing disguise. Can Destiny make herself look like you?"

Comet nodded, his tail twitching. "But no disguise will help her if the dark horses find her. She has been far away from the Stone of Power for so long that they are able to see through her magic. I must look for my sister. Will you help me?"

"Of course I will," Preeti said at once, not thinking how difficult that could be.

She suddenly remembered the news announcement about how the weather had brought everything to a standstill. It had been bad enough making her way through the deep snow to get to the barn. Tramping through it for hours in search of a lost pony would be impossible.

She told Comet her worries. "The snow's really thick outside, and it's very hard to walk in it. Maybe I could ask Mom and Dad to help—" she began.

"No! I am sorry, but you cannot tell anyone about me or what I have told you," Comet snorted, his eyes serious. "You must promise me, Preeti."

Preeti chewed her bottom lip. She felt disappointed that she couldn't tell her parents about the amazing pony. She was sure they would have kept his secret— even if Viren definitely wouldn't have been able to! But Comet was looking at her with a mixture of complete trust and confidence, and she found herself nodding.

"All right then," she said hesitantly, prepared to agree if it would keep Comet and Destiny safe from their enemies.

"Thank you for keeping my secret." Comet gave a soft blow and reached forward to gently nuzzle her coat sleeve. "And do not worry. I have my magic to help us when we search for Destiny."

"That's . . . um, okay then," Preeti said, intrigued. She couldn't imagine

what sort of "help" he meant, but she
guessed it was going to be something
really unusual.

As she reached up to stroke his satiny
cheek, a proud smile spread across her
face. A magic pony had chosen her to be
his friend. How amazing was that?

Comet's ears swiveled, and he turned
his head toward the door. At the same
time, Preeti heard a noise behind her.
She spun around to see her little brother

brushing snow off his coat as he stepped
into the barn.

Catching sight of Preeti and Comet,
Viren froze.

"Where did that pony come from?" he
gasped, his big brown eyes like saucers.

Chapter
THREE

Preeti racked her brains as she tried
to come up with something. What could
she say to Viren? How could she explain
Comet's presence?

"I found Comet in . . . um . . .
the garden," she began. "He must have
wandered in . . . from that empty field
next to the road or something," she went
on, gaining confidence as she remembered

that ponies were sometimes tethered there. "Comet looked cold and hungry, so I decided to bring him into the barn."

"He was pretty clever to come here, wasn't he?" Viren went up to Comet and stroked his nose. "Poor thing. I bet you couldn't get to the grass, because of all the snow." He turned back to Preeti. "How come you know his name?"

"I don't," Preeti fibbed. "I called him Comet because . . . I've . . . um, always liked that name."

"I like it, too. It suits him," Viren decided. "Comet can stay here, can't he? It's nice and warm, and we can feed him straw and stuff."

"Ponies eat hay. Straw's just for their beds—" Preeti started explaining when Comet neighed eagerly.

"I would like to live in here, very much. It is a safe place." He pricked his ears as he swept the barn with keen eyes.

Preeti did a double take. What was Comet doing? He had just given himself away in front of Viren!

But her little brother appeared not to have noticed anything odd. It was very strange.

Trying to gather her wits, she said, "Well—I don't suppose anyone's going to come looking for Comet until the roads are clear. And he does need somewhere to shelter from the—"

"So we *can* keep him? Cool!" Viren interrupted. "Great! I'll go and tell Mom and Dad and Grandma. I'm going to get a brush so I can groom him. We've got a pet pony! We've got a pet pony!" he chanted in an annoying singsong voice, jumping around.

Before Preeti could protest that Comet was actually *her* friend and that he definitely wasn't anyone's pet, especially not Viren's, her little brother had slipped outside. She went to the door and saw him scuttling back to the house through the tracks she'd made earlier.

"I'm going to tell everyone about Comet. I can't wait to see the looks on their faces!" he shouted over his shoulder to her.

Preeti gave a sigh and tried not to feel too disappointed. She'd been really excited about doing that herself. Even if she could only say that Comet was a normal pony who had turned up looking for food and shelter.

She turned back to the magic pony. "Now that Viren's decided that you belong to both of us, we'll never get rid of him. He'll be trailing around with us all the time."

"Viren seems like a nice little boy," Comet neighed.

"But he can be a real pest," Preeti said, shaking her head slowly. "Everyone lets him do whatever he wants. So he's totally spoiled." But something else was bothering her. "How come he didn't seem to hear you speak to me just now?"

Comet wrinkled his lips in amusement. "I used my magic so that only you will be able to see and hear me. To anyone else, I will seem like a normal pony."

"Really?" Preeti felt herself cheering up. Viren might have laid claim to Comet, but only she had been trusted with her new friend's wonderful secret!

"Comet had better live in our barn until the weather breaks and we can find out who owns him," Mrs. Nimesh was saying as Preeti came back into the house. "I know it's not an ideal stable, but it'll only be for a short time." She smiled at her daughter. "It looks like you have a pony to take care of, after all, Preeti!"

"Yay! Isn't it great?" Preeti felt her grin stretch from ear to ear.

"And I do, too. Comet's half mine!" Viren insisted.

Preeti wisely kept silent.

Her mom went to make a quick phone call to the local pet center and leave their address and phone number, in case Comet's owner turned up.

Preeti was totally confident that no one was going to claim her secret magical friend.

"We're keeping the pony. We're keeping the pony!" Viren pretended to be riding around the kitchen. Clicking his tongue, he made clopping noises as he galloped out of the kitchen and thudded up the stairs.

Preeti decided to go back down to the barn to tell Comet the good news about him being allowed to stay. Besides, she wanted to settle him in properly. She was halfway there when she heard a familiar voice.

"Wait for me! I'm coming, too. I want to help!" Viren insisted.

"Okay, then, but you have to do as I say," she told him.

He frowned. "Why?"

"Because I'm older and I know how to look after ponies," Preeti said firmly. "Deal?"

Viren groaned, but when he saw that she was serious, he shrugged. "Deal."

Comet looked up as they came in. "Greetings, Preeti. Greetings, Viren," he snorted.

"Hi, Comet!" Viren sang out, rushing straight over to stroke him.

Preeti smiled at Comet. "We've come to make you a comfortable stable."

She showed Viren how to spread a thick layer of straw to make a cozy bed.

"Easy-peasy!" He gathered armfuls of straw, but he dropped more than half of it and left wisps and clumps all over the floor.

Preeti decided that it was easier to just let him get on with it and then clean up afterward. She knew from experience that her brother would get upset if she pointed out that he was making a mess.

"Right. Finished!" Viren said proudly a few minutes later. He dusted off his hands. "I'm going to build a snowman now! Come and help me, Preeti."

"I still have to finish up in here. You go ahead and I'll follow you in a minute," she said.

"Well, hurry up then."

Once her brother had gone outside, Preeti filled a bucket with water and then found some old netting and managed to rig up a makeshift hay net.

Comet nibbled at the hay with his strong young teeth. "It is very warm and safe here. Thank you," he whinnied.

"You're welcome!" Preeti smiled, pleased that Comet liked his cozy new stable.

"Preeti! Where are you?" Viren bawled impatiently from the garden. "I'm getting bored by myself."

"I'm just cleaning up!" Preeti called to him. She sighed. *What a mess!*

She was just about to start tackling it when she felt a strange tingling sensation flowing down to the ends of her fingers. Bright violet sparks ignited in Comet's silky mouse-brown coat, and his dark gray mane crackled with tiny lightning bolts of power.

Preeti's eyes widened. Something very strange was about to happen.

She watched in amazement as every last scrap of the scattered straw twitched up into the air. *Swoosh! Crackle!* It swirled around for a few seconds before gathering together and forming the shape of a large straw robot. *Rustle!* He marched across the

barn to where the straw bales were stored
and jumped on top of them.

With a soft whispering sound, the
straw robot collapsed into a neat heap,
just as every last bright spark faded from
Comet's coat.

"Wow! That was amazing!" Preeti said.
"It would have taken me ages to clean all
that up. Thanks, Comet."

"You are welcome. Now you can go
and have fun in the snow, too." Comet
leaned forward to push his satiny nose into
her hands.

Preeti's heart melted as the magic
pony huffed warm grass-scented breath
over her fingers. She felt a surge of
fondness for him. Comet hadn't been here
for long, but she already loved him to
pieces.

Chapter FOUR

As Preeti made her way through the garden, it finally stopped snowing. The sky was milk-white above the rooftops.

Viren was on the small lawn outside the sitting-room window. He was puffing and panting as he piled armfuls of snow into a big mound.

"That took you forever," he complained moodily. "I bet you wanted to stay there with Comet, so you had him all to yourself. He's mine, too, you know!"

"Actually, I was cleaning up the mess *you* made!" Preeti exclaimed. She bit back an even ruder reply as she silently counted to ten. "Never mind. Let's build this snowman," she said more calmly, bending down to scoop up some snow.

Thump! A snowball hit her on the arm.

"What a shot!" Viren crowed.

"Hey!" Grinning, Preeti threw one back at him.

Suddenly, they were pelting each other with snowballs. In all the fun of the fight, Preeti forgot for a while to be mad at her brother. Her breath was steaming out in the cold air, and her cheeks began to glow.

"Truce!" she gasped finally as another snowball hit her on the head, and powdery snow dribbled inside her coat collar. "We'd better stop now or we'll never finish this snowman!"

"Okay," Viren agreed. "But I won!" His cheeks were flushed, too, and his dark eyes shone mischievously.

"If you say so," Preeti said.

"I do!" he shot back, having the last word.

They made a big pile of snow and patted it into shape. Soon they had the snowman's body. Preeti showed her little brother how to roll a snowball around so that it gathered snow, and it soon grew to the right shape and size for a head.

"Should we give him a face?" she asked.

"Not yet," Viren said, his eyes sparkling. "We have to make some legs."

"Legs?" Preeti raised her eyebrows; then she remembered his earlier plan to make a snow dinosaur.

They made four stumpy legs and put them on so they stuck straight out from the snowman's body. They looked a little weird, but Viren nodded in satisfaction. He began forming two small triangular ears on the top of the head and shaping the face into a longish muzzle.

"That's the funniest-looking dinosaur I've ever seen!" Preeti said, starting to laugh.

Viren frowned. "It's not a dinosaur.
Can't you tell what it is?"

"Give me a clue!" Preeti said, putting
her head to one side.

"Just a minute." Viren went and
scrabbled in the snow beneath a small
tree and then returned with a handful
of twigs. He jabbed a clump of them
between the lumpy ears and placed the

rest of them in a line that marched down the back of the neck.

"Now can you tell what it is?" he asked.

"A snow alien?" Preeti spluttered.

Viren scowled with annoyance. He put his hands on his hips. "No, you dummy. It's a snow pony! *Obviously!*"

"*Obviously*—not!" Preeti replied—it looked like a very odd pony to her.

"I've made a friend for Comet. I'm going to tell him," Viren said, heading back toward the barn.

"I'll come with you," Preeti said, breathing on her gloves to warm her cold fingers. "Then I think we should go and get some hot chocolate. I'm freezing."

"Okay. Maybe Comet's cold, too. We could bring him some hot chocolate."

"Ponies only drink water," she told him,

not really concentrating. "And he'll be fine in the barn. He said that he likes it there, because it's cozy and warm."

"How did Comet tell you that?" Viren scoffed. "Ponies can't talk!"

"Um . . . no, of course they can't. I was . . . er, just thinking that's what he'd say if he *could* talk," Preeti said hastily, realizing that she was going to have be more careful about keeping Comet's secret.

"It's so cool having a pony to look after," Viren declared excitedly. "I'm going to spend every moment I can out here with Comet. I might bring my sleeping bag out so I can sit and read to him. And I could . . ."

Preeti's heart sank as Viren chattered on. The way her little brother was taking over completely was really annoying and presented her with a big problem.

"I can't see how I'm going to slip away by myself so we can search for Destiny," she whispered to Comet. "He's even talking about camping out in the barn!"

Comet's deep-violet eyes twinkled, and he swished his gray tail. "I believe in you, Preeti. I know you will think of a way," he neighed confidently.

Chapter FIVE

As evening fell, the snow began falling
again, and it soon covered the tracks Preeti
and Viren had made through the garden
earlier. The news on TV showed pictures
of people stranded on highways, and
planes unable to take off from airports.
Everything was at a standstill.

"The trouble is, we're not used to
this weather in this part of the country,"

Mrs. Nimesh said, switching channels with the remote control. "If we were, there'd be special measures in place to deal with it, like enough snowplows to clear the main roads."

Grandma glanced out of the sitting-room window at the snow pony on the lawn. It seemed to glow faintly in the moonlight. "He is very beautiful. He could be there for a long time in this freezing weather," she commented.

Preeti was curled up in a chair, reading

a book of pony stories. She loved the
feeling of being warm and cozy inside
the house when everything was white
and frozen outside. Comet was safe in the
barn, and there would be no school for
a while, so she could spend a ton of time
with him.

If only she could think of a way
of distracting Viren for a few hours,
everything would be perfect.

She looked up to smile at her grandma
and saw that she looked a bit worried. "Is
something wrong?" she asked.

"I was just thinking about Mr. Linford.
He lives alone and his relatives are very
far away. I hope he will be all right." Mr.
Linford was an elderly gentleman whom
Grandma had met while she was giving
lessons in Indian cooking at the local

community center. They often met to talk and share a pot of tea.

"Does he live very far away?" Preeti asked.

"No. It is only three minutes away by car. But, of course, I cannot drive to see him."

"Why don't you walk there and visit him?" Preeti suggested. She had a sudden brain wave. "Maybe Viren will go with you."

Grandma smiled. "That is a kind thought. I think I will call Mr. Linford now." She left the room and Preeti soon heard her talking to her friend.

"How is he?" she asked when her grandma returned a few minutes later.

"Mr. Linford said he is fine for now," Grandma told her. "But he is rather

worried that he cannot get out of his
house to get to the store for milk and
bread. Perhaps we could visit him, in a day
or two, and take him some groceries?"

Mr. Nimesh looked up from where he
sat reading his newspaper. "The sidewalk is
very icy, Mother. Please take great care if
you go out walking."

Grandma nodded worriedly. "Ice is a
problem. Well, perhaps this cold spell will
not last. Those TV weathermen do not
know everything." She shook her head
slowly as she went into the kitchen.

Preeti watched her go. She hadn't
really thought about the problems that
snow could bring. She realized now that
this weather wasn't fun for everyone,
especially older people.

She read for a bit longer and then

stifled a yawn as she closed her book. It was getting late, and she decided to go and see Comet before she went upstairs to bed. Viren had left the room a little while ago, and she thought she had heard him going upstairs. He was probably already in bed, asleep.

But the moment Preeti went into the garden, she spotted fresh tracks in the snow that led to the barn.

Viren hadn't gone to bed at all. He had sneaked out again to see Comet. She couldn't suppress a prickle of resentment. It was starting to look as if she'd never be alone with Comet.

Then she had an idea. There was only one thing to do.

Preeti woke with a start to find the bedroom still dark and the house silent.

She dressed quickly, being extra careful not to make any noise, and crept downstairs. Grabbing the nearest coat, she threw it on and then thrust her feet into a pair of worn old boots before tiptoeing outside.

The bright moonlight cast midnight-blue shadows across the snow and made it easy to see as she went down to the barn.

Comet gave a soft neigh of welcome as she slipped inside. "You are alone?"

"Yes, at last! Hi, Comet." Preeti reached up to stroke his silky cheek. "We've got lots of time to go out looking for Destiny before everyone wakes up! Let's go!"

"Thank you. Climb onto my back, Preeti." Comet tossed his head with eagerness, his eyes flashing.

Preeti nervously climbed up and sat astride him. It had been forever since her last riding lesson, and anyway, she wasn't used to riding bareback. But the moment she twined her hands in his thick gray mane, Comet's warm magic seemed to spread around her, and she felt completely safe and secure.

Comet moved forward and in two strides reached the closed barn door.

"Wait! I'll open it . . . ," Preeti began.

Then she gasped as, with a flash of bright violet sparks, Comet gave a mighty leap and floated *through* the door in a swoosh of glittering mist that left the door unchanged. They were soon galloping across the snow, the magic pony's shining hooves barely brushing the white surface and leaving no tracks.

Chapter
SIX

Preeti laughed aloud with delight as
they sped along in the silver moonlight,
with snowflakes gently falling around
them. Excitement raced through her.
Comet was amazing to ride, so smooth
and thrilling. His magic surrounded them,
and no matter how fast they raced along,
she felt perfectly safe.

The magic pony's head turned left and

right as he rushed onward. His keen eyes
were searching for any sign that Destiny
had come this way.

"Hold tight!" Comet warned.

He flashed over silent roads in the
blink of an eye, and stores and houses
passed by in a blur. They shot past factories
and buildings until they came to the edge
of town. An expanse of snow-covered
fields stretched ahead of them.

"Look!" Preeti cried after a while,
pointing to a field with a shelter at one
end. Tractor marks led across the snow to
a bale of hay that four hardy little ponies
with thick winter coats were eating.
"Maybe Destiny is disguised as one of
those."

Comet checked his stride and slowed
as he cantered over to investigate. But

none of the little group was Destiny. He
trotted away sadly.

"I hope Destiny is hiding somewhere
safe," Comet nickered, his head drooping.
"The dark horses will steal her magic if
they can."

Preeti could see that he was badly
missing his twin sister. "We'll go out
looking every night," she promised.
"Maybe it will be easier to find her with
no people or cars around. Everywhere is

deserted because of the snow."

"That is true." Comet gave a long soft blow as he looked around with renewed interest. His breath hung in the freezing air like twinkling clouds of steam.

Slowing his stride, he moved at a gentler pace. Preeti rose to the trot as they checked out some woods. Soon they emerged opposite a deep railway cutting before moving onward again. But they didn't see any other ponies.

Preeti noticed a faint rosy light beginning to wash across the sky. Dawn was approaching.

"I think we'd better head home. Grandma gets up really early," she said reluctantly.

"Very well." Comet took a circular route that eventually brought them back across the fields and to the road leading into town.

It began to snow more heavily, making it difficult to see far ahead. Preeti shivered, wishing now that she'd taken the time to put on her warmest coat with the fake fur–trimmed hood and her newest boots.

The coat she'd picked up in a hurry was a very light spring one.

"You are cold," Comet whickered.

Preeti felt a faint tingling feeling in her fingertips as Comet's mane twinkled with tiny violet sparkles. A clear bubble spread around her, keeping her warm and dry. The snowflakes melted as they touched the bubble's surface, so she could also see where they were going.

"That's much better. Thanks, Comet." Suddenly, Preeti caught a movement from the corner of her eye. "Hold on. Look! Over there. In that ditch."

"Is it Destiny?" Comet neighed urgently, rocking onto his back legs as he halted.

Preeti clung tightly. Just beyond the roadside, the ground sloped sharply away.

Comet stood looking down into the ditch, which seemed to be filled by a big lumpy snowdrift. But there was no pony sheltering there.

"What's that?" Preeti frowned, puzzled, staring at the pile of snow. "It looks like part of a door and back window." Her eyes widened in shock. "Oh my goodness! There's a car under there! And I think someone's inside it!"

Chapter
SEVEN

"We have to help!" Preeti cried.

Comet nodded. "Lean against me. We
will climb down together."

Quickly dismounting, Preeti put one
arm around Comet's neck and braced
herself against his strong shoulder as they
slid and stumbled down the deep bank
until they reached the ditch.

Luckily the car seemed to have just slid

down and landed the right way up. The front of it was sloping slightly downward.

Preeti began frantically trying to clear snow from the side windows. "If I can just brush some of this away, we'll be able to see inside the car!" But in just seconds, her hands were numb with cold.

"I will help," Comet neighed beside her.

Preeti felt another warm prickling sensation flowing to the ends of her fingers as he huffed out a sparkly breath that twinkled with thousands of tiny rainbow stars. The glittering mist swirled around the car for a few seconds and swept up the entire covering of snow, which then fell far away in the field beyond.

As the car was revealed, Preeti saw two faces looking out at them. It was a

woman and a little girl who looked about
Viren's age. They were huddled together
under layers of coats as they tried to keep
warm.

"Are you okay?" Preeti called, tapping
on the window.

The woman nodded. She leaned
over to speak to her through the closed
window. "We're not hurt, just a bit cold,"
she shouted. "I called for help on my

cell. We've been waiting here for hours. I think a big truck or something went past a while back, but it didn't see us. I didn't want to leave Emily and go up to the road to flag it down. I stayed here and tried to keep us both warm."

"That was the best thing to do," Comet whinnied to Preeti.

The woman in the car did a double take as she heard pony noises. She peered over Preeti's shoulder and seemed to see Comet for the first time in the thick swirling snow. "Is that your pony? But . . . how come . . .? What . . .?"

Preeti thought quickly. "We're . . . er . . . helping the . . . rescue team," she said vaguely. "Don't worry. Help will be here soon."

The woman nodded gratefully. "We

have a chance of being seen, now that
you've cleared the snow away, though
I don't know how you did it. And it's
strange, but it feels a lot warmer in here
now."

Preeti smiled with relief when a
moment later she saw Comet prick up
his ears. Seconds later, Preeti heard it,
too: the chugging rumble of a snowplow.
Powerful searchlights penetrated the
blinding snow as the big truck appeared
around a bend.

The woman and her daughter, Emily,
would be fine now, but she and Comet
had to leave before anyone else knew
that they'd been there. She didn't want
her mom and dad finding out about her
midnight ride.

Comet leaned forward to gently

snuffle her hair. "We must leave now," he neighed. The sky was much lighter and the sound of the truck was getting closer.

Preeti leaned close to the window to speak to the woman one final time. "We have to go now. Bye!" she called, backing away.

"Wait! How can I thank you . . .?" the woman shouted.

But her voice faded as Preeti turned and held onto Comet again, and they climbed out of the ditch. Once they were back on the road, she mounted again.

"Well done, Comet!" she praised.

Bending forward, she heard the wind whistling past them outside the magical bubble as Comet galloped flat out. The blizzard raged on, but she was safe and warm. In the early-morning light, the swirling snowflakes were tinted pale apricot and gold. Once again, Preeti felt the heart-stopping thrill of riding the magic pony. And she knew she would remember this amazing night for the rest of her life.

Back at the barn, she rubbed Comet down and made sure he had fresh water

and hay. "You were incredible tonight, Comet!" she told him, stroking his velvety nose. "Those people in the car will be rescued because of you."

His deep-violet eyes gleamed. "I am glad I could help."

"You deserve a rest. You've been riding hard," she said fondly, stranding his mane through her fingers.

"I would gallop all day without a rest, if it meant I would find Destiny," he told her, blowing out a long breath through his flared nostrils. "You are lucky that your little brother is safe and here with you."

Preeti hadn't thought about it like that. Viren was such a pest that she sometimes wished she were an only child, but she really did love him.

"I know you miss Destiny a lot," she

said gently. She put her arms around his neck and laid her cheek against his warm silky coat. "I wish we could find her, too. And then maybe you could both live here with me? I could ask Mom and Dad if we could make part of the barn into a proper stable."

Comet shook his head slowly. "I am afraid that is not possible. Destiny and I must go back to our Lightning Herd on Rainbow Mist Island."

"Oh." Preeti sighed. She supposed she knew that already, but she didn't want to believe it. It was just too painful to think of her special friend leaving. She decided to push it to the back of her mind.

"I'll see you later," she said as she went out and closed the barn door behind her.

From now on, she was going to make sure that she enjoyed every single moment spent with Comet.

Chapter EIGHT

"It is strange to think that we will celebrate *Holi* in a few days," Grandma commented the following day. She was in the kitchen, making coconut sweets. "Who would think it would snow so heavily in March?"

"I know, it doesn't feel like we should be celebrating the coming of spring," Preeti replied. She was helping to make

the delicious sweets they usually gave away
as gifts when visiting friends and relatives.

Mrs. Nimesh came in from her office
to have a coffee break. "You two look
busy," she said, smiling, looking at the trays
of colorful treats. "So many? Who will eat
them all? I think it might be a rather quiet
Holi this year."

Preeti felt disappointed, as she thought

her mom could be right. The snow was keeping everyone from traveling.

She loved it when everyone gathered together at festival times. *Holi* was particularly fun because it was associated with Lord Krishna, who was famous for making trouble and playing tricks on his friends. It was a time for everyone to do the same. People wore their oldest clothes and threw brightly colored powders at each other.

Viren enjoyed it especially, because he was allowed to get really messy without being yelled at! But this year it looked as if their family would be celebrating alone because of the dangerously icy roads.

"Couldn't we have a party here?" Preeti pleaded, looking at her mom. "Some of our friends live close enough to walk. We could make a big bonfire in the snow. Dad's got lots of dry wood in the barn. It would be fun and we could keep warm playing games and dancing."

Her mom looked thoughtful. "It would mean a lot of work, cooking and preparing party food."

"I'll help!" Preeti offered at once.

Mrs. Nimesh nodded. "All right. Why not? I will go and make some phone calls, right away."

"Yay!" Preeti cried delightedly.

Viren wandered in playing a video game. It was making twittering and popping noises as he pressed the buttons with his thumbs. He grabbed a few of the cooling coconut squares, and popped a piece in his mouth.

"Mmm. You make the best sweets

in the whole world, Grandma!" he
exclaimed, rubbing his tummy.

"You silly boy! You will not get
around me like that!" Grandma ruffled
her grandson's curly dark hair, but she was
smiling with pleasure. "But that's enough
now, or you will not eat your lunch," she
scolded fondly.

Viren turned to Preeti. "Who's Mom
calling?" Preeti told him about the party
they were planning. "Cool! A snow party.
Comet can come, too. We'll powder him
with all different colors. He'll love *Holi*!"
Plunking himself on the sofa at the far
end of the eat-in kitchen, Viren switched
on the TV.

Preeti was rolling the sweet mixture
into small balls when she heard the
newscaster's voice floating toward her.

". . . a woman who was rescued in the early hours of yesterday morning after her car skidded into a ditch has reported a mysterious ghostly sighting of a girl and a pony. Apparently the girl spoke to her. The driver of a snowplow also glimpsed them briefly in his headlights, before the girl and her pony disappeared without a trace. If anyone has any information . . ."

"Oh no!" Preeti murmured under

her breath. She felt herself growing hot and was sure her face must have been bright red. "I have to go and . . . um . . . do something in the barn," she mumbled hastily, washing her sticky hands. "See you later!" she called over her shoulder as she hightailed it out of the kitchen.

Grandma and Viren didn't respond. They were glued to the TV, spellbound by the story of the ghostly girl and her pony.

"Phew! I didn't expect to hear about us on the news!" Preeti said to Comet. She had removed his soiled bedding and spread fresh straw, and was now giving the guinea pigs some pieces of cucumber for a treat. Chandra and Surya were making excited grunting noises as they snuffled and licked cucumber juice from her fingers. "It's a good thing that woman and the snowplow driver didn't get a good look at us, or I'd be in deep trouble with Mom and Dad now!"

With Comet looking after her, Preeti knew she couldn't have been in safer hands. But her parents wouldn't see it like that. She didn't want to try to explain what she was doing riding around at night.

Comet's gray mane swung forward as he nodded in agreement. "When we go out looking for Destiny again, I will use my magic to make us both invisible."

"You can do that? Wow! That's *so* cool! Then I don't need to worry about anyone seeing us."

It had been so amazing to ride Comet. She had loved their exciting snowy adventure. "I'd like to go out with you again right now," she said, although she knew it was far too risky, especially with Viren likely to pop his head into the barn at any moment. "Though I'd better wait and slip out when everyone's asleep, like last night."

But by a stroke of luck, Preeti found herself with time on her hands that afternoon. Grandma was walking over to visit her friend Mr. Linford, and Mom and Viren had gone with her. Her dad was at the hospital, so the house was empty for once.

"I pretended I had some homework to do," she told Comet. "So I could stay here. Now we can go out looking for Destiny."

"Thank you, Preeti." Comet's eyes flashed, and he pawed the floor with one front hoof. "Climb onto my back again."

Preeti didn't need to be told twice. As they galloped away from the barn, she showed him the way to a different part of town. Once again, Comet's shining hooves skimmed the surface of the snow and their invisible passing left no trail.

The snowplows had been busy, and traffic was beginning to move very slowly on the main road. Preeti saw lots of snow-covered cars left in driveways and parked along the side of the road. Ice and snow blocked all the side streets.

"There's a park just over there with lots of places where Destiny might hide," Preeti said, pointing.

Comet pricked his ears hopefully.

As they drew closer, they could hear shouts and laughter. About thirty kids of all ages were playing in the snow. More of

them were riding their sleds down a steep hill.

Preeti and Comet rode between the trees and snow-covered bushes, keeping a sharp eye out for any signs of a pony. At first, Preeti found it strange that no one paid them any attention, but she soon got used to it.

Being invisible was a lot of fun!

They investigated an area with clipped hedges, but found nothing. Comet snorted and they rode on toward a large frozen lake.

Ducks and geese waddled on the surface, and noisy seagulls wheeled overhead. A forest of tall dried reeds stuck up through the snow along a stretch of the lakeside, providing enough cover for a lost pony. But once again they had no luck.

Galloping away from the park, Comet headed toward a shopping center.

"Let's try over there," Preeti said, squeezing him on, as she pointed to a superstore with a large parking lot. "Maybe it would be warmer behind the store. A pony could find shelter there."

Comet nodded, flicking up his tail with eagerness.

But he had barely begun to cross the snow-covered parking lot when Preeti felt him stiffen. As her magic pony friend

stopped and leaned down to look at the
ground, she looked down, too.

In front of them both and stretching
all the way across the parking lot was
a faint line of softly glowing violet
hoofprints.

"Destiny! She came this way!" Comet
neighed excitedly.

Preeti felt a pang. Did that mean her
friend was leaving right now? "Are . . . are
you going follow her?" she asked anxiously.

Comet shook his head. "No. There
is no point. This trail is not fresh. But it
proves that Destiny was here. She cannot
be too far away. When she is very close, I
will be able to hear her hoofbeats."

"Will I be able to hear them, too?"
Preeti asked.

"Yes. But only if you are riding me, or

we are together," he explained in a soft neigh. "And I may have to leave suddenly, without saying good-bye, to catch up with her."

Preeti bit her lip during this reminder that Comet could not stay with her forever. She swallowed hard as tears threatened to well up, knowing that she would never be ready to lose her special magic friend.

Chapter
NINE

After searching for a while longer, with no more signs of Destiny, Preeti and Comet turned toward home. Preeti wasn't sure how long Grandma, Mom, and Viren would stay at Mr. Linford's house, and she hoped they would get back before they returned.

On the way, they cut through some narrow lanes and alleyways and finally emerged at the far side of the park, a short way from the frozen lake. A group of people were on the shore. As they drew closer, shouts rang out.

"A little boy's fallen through the ice!" a girl cried.

Preeti tightened her hands on Comet's mane and looked toward the commotion. She had a bad feeling about this. More people were running toward the lake, where a tiny shape out on the ice was waving its arms around.

As the magic pony checked his stride, Preeti frowned. There was something familiar about that figure. Then her heart missed a beat.

"It's Viren!" she gasped.

What was her little brother doing here?

Comet didn't hesitate. "Hold tight!"

He launched himself into the air in a mighty leap. Seconds later he landed lightly on the lake's frozen surface, in the center of the reed bed. A foot away, Viren's head and shoulders were sticking up through a hole in the ice as he tried to pull himself out.

Quickly dismounting, Preeti crawled forward and knelt at the edge of the reeds.

"Hang on, Viren!" she gasped.

"Preeti? Is that you?" His frightened dark eyes widened in shock as he looked around, trying to see where her voice had come from. "Where . . . where are you?" he gulped, his teeth chattering.

Preeti remembered that she and Comet were still invisible. What was she to do? How could she explain her sudden appearance? There was no blizzard to hide them this time. She felt torn. She had to help her brother, but she had promised to keep Comet's secret.

Preeti made up her mind.

"Comet! Make me visible, please!" she whispered.

The magic pony's wise eyes gleamed. "Very well."

Preeti felt the familiar warm tingling feeling flow down her fingers and saw bright sparks igniting in Comet's coat as a shimmering multicolored mist swirled around them. The magical rainbow fog spread out across the lake's surface, making the ice safe and hiding them from the people on the shore.

Preeti lay down and inched herself forward onto the thicker ice. "Don't worry! I'm here!" she called to Viren.

His face crumpled with relief. "Preeti!"

Almost there! Preeti kicked out strongly with her feet and skidded toward him. *Yes!* Her fingers closed on a wet sleeve. "Got you!"

She took a firm hold, pulled with all her strength, and hauled Viren out. He collapsed in a wet heap on the ice beside her.

For a moment she lay there, panting. Viren was shivering badly.

A magical fleecy blanket of shimmering rainbow mist settled warmly

around them both. "Quickly, while he is
still confused. Lift him onto my back,"
Comet neighed softly.

Preeti was worried that Viren would
be too heavy for her. But as she scooped
him up in her arms, she found that he
was as light as a feather, and she mounted
Comet easily.

With a burst of violet sparkles, Comet made them all invisible before he sprang into the air. His giant leap carried them high above the frozen lake. Then, landing on the shore, he bore them home at nearly the speed of light.

Preeti hardly had time to catch her breath before she found herself inside the warm barn. Moments later, she was standing beside Comet, looking down at Viren, who lay on the clean straw.

Her brother sat up, rubbing his eyes as if he was waking from a dream. "What . . . what just happened?" Viren blinked up at her in surprise. "I . . . I don't get it. How did I get back here?"

"I managed to grab you and pull you out of the water. You were in a bit of a daze, but you managed to walk home

with me," Preeti improvised quickly.
"It was lucky I was at the park and saw
you fall through the ice. What were you
doing there, anyway? You know you're
not allowed to go off by yourself. If
Mom and Dad find out about this, you're
toast!"

Viren's face clouded. "You won't tell
them, will you?" he pleaded.

"I haven't decided yet. Why *were* you
at the park, anyway?" she asked him.

Viren hung his head and looked
sorry for himself. "After I got back from
Grandma's friend's house, I came to see
Comet. But he wasn't in the barn! When
I couldn't find you, either, I went to look
for him by myself. I thought he might go
to the park because there was grass there
to eat."

Preeti nodded. It kind of made sense.

She felt a stir of guilt. This was partly her fault. She could have invited Viren to help her look after Comet, instead of always trying to avoid him. And maybe if she and Comet had come back earlier, none of this would have happened. Viren had been brave to try to find the lost pony all by himself.

"What about you? Why were you there?" Viren demanded. "I thought you were supposed to be doing your homework."

"I was. But I finished it. So I went for a walk," Preeti fibbed. "Anyway, never mind that. The main thing is that you're okay now."

Viren didn't challenge her. He gave a subdued nod and then stood up and brushed himself down. A grin spread over his face. "Comet came back, didn't he? So that's all right! Hc likes living here with us!" Viren reached up to put both arms around Comet's neck and buried his face against the warm gray-brown skin.

The magic pony swung his head down and gently butted the little boy's arm.

"Yes. I like it here," he neighed softly, although Viren only heard normal pony noises.

Preeti waited until Viren had finished cuddling Comet. She was pleased to see that the color had come back to her brother's face and that he seemed none the worse for his frightening experience on the ice.

"I think you should go and get out of those wet clothes before Mom starts asking awkward questions, don't you?" she suggested gently.

"Okay!" Viren didn't need to be told twice. "Thanks for not tattling, sis!" He rushed at her and gave her a swift damp hug before running out.

Preeti stared after him. A smile curved her lips. Viren could be annoying sometimes, but he could be sweet, too. Besides, he was the only brother she had.

Chapter
TEN

At last it was *Holi* Eve. The evening was clear and very cold and still.

A colorful feast was spread out in the house. Preeti's mouth watered at all the delicious smells. She stood looking into the garden, where she could see Viren and her dad putting the finishing touches to the bonfire.

Her brother saw her looking and

waved. Preeti smiled and waved back. They had been getting along better since what had happened in the park.

She decided to quickly slip down to the barn. This might be the only chance she got to spend a few moments alone with Comet this evening. She helped herself to a big rosy apple from the fruit bowl in the kitchen. After quickly slicing it, she slipped it into her pocket.

Earlier, she had pushed candles into the snow to encircle the small lawn close to the house. As she walked past, their light flickered onto the snow pony that she and Viren had made over a week ago.

Grandma was right. In this freezing weather, it had lasted well.

Preeti reached the barn and went inside to where the magic pony was waiting. At the sight of him, a warm glow spread through her. He was her special secret, and she'd never tell anyone about him.

"Greetings, Preeti," Comet whinnied, turning to look at her.

She smiled as she reached up to stroke him in the sensitive place between his eyes. "I've got something for you." She took out the apple and fed it to him slice by slice.

Comet crunched it up in his strong teeth. "Delicious."

"Our friends and relatives will be here soon," she told him. "I can't wait for them to see you. In a little while we'll say prayers and light the fire. Then we throw offering of coconuts, popcorn, and rice into the flames. You'll love celebrating *Holi* with us!"

Comet nodded, his deep-violet eyes shining. He knew Destiny would have loved it, too.

Preeti smiled at him. She went over to the rabbit and guinea pig cages where there was a pile of old blankets, which she used to cover them at night. She shook out the cleanest one and brought it over.

"This will keep you warm," she said, placing the blanket on Comet's back.

"Thank you, Preeti," he neighed as she led him out of the barn.

Sounds of laughter and voices raised in greeting reached them. She caught a glimpse of jewel-bright saris through the lit-up windows. Viren was running excitedly through garden toward the house.

"Everyone's here!" Preeti exclaimed excitedly. "Come on, Comet, let's go and meet them."

Comet had taken only a few steps when he suddenly froze. Preeti heard a sound she'd been both hoping for and dreading.

The hollow sound of hooves galloping overhead.

"Destiny!"

Comet ran straight at the ranch-style

garden gate. He sailed over it and into the alleyway, following the magical hoofbeats, which sounded louder and closer.

Preeti ran after him. Her heart raced as she opened the gate and flung herself through it. She knew that this time Comet was leaving for good, and she was going to have to be very strong and let him go.

There was a violet flash, and a twinkling rainbow mist floated down around Comet. He stood there in his true form, a grey-brown pony no longer, but a magnificent magic pony with a noble head, a cream coat, and spreading gold-feathered wings. His golden mane and tail flowed down in shimmering silky strands.

"Comet!" Preeti gasped. She had almost forgotten how beautiful he was.

"I . . . I hope you catch Destiny. I'll never forget you!" she said, her voice breaking.

Comet turned to look at her for one last time, his eyes clouded with sadness. "I will not forget you, either. You have been a good friend. Ride well and true," he said in a deep musical neigh.

There was a final flash of violet light, and a silent burst of rainbow sparkles drifted down around Preeti in frozen snowflakes that tinkled as they hit the ground. Preeti gulped back tears, feeling as if her heart would break. She had known he would have to leave one day, but she couldn't believe it had happened so fast.

Something glittered in the snow. It was a single shimmering gold wing feather. Reaching down, she picked it up. It tingled against her palm as it faded to a cream color. She slipped it into her pocket, knowing she would treasure it always as a reminder of the wonderful adventure she had shared with the magic pony.

Then, as she turned and went back

into the garden, she saw Viren running
toward her. "I came to get you! Where's
Comet?" he cried.

"His . . . his owner turned up and
took him away in a truck," Preeti said,
wiping her eyes.

"Oh." Viren's small face crumpled.
"I'm going to miss him a lot."

She put her arms around him,
suddenly feeling like a grown-up big sister.
It was a new feeling, and she kind of liked
it. "I know. Me too," she said, wiping her
eyes. "But Comet never belonged to us,
not really. We always knew he'd go back
to the family who loved him as much as
we did." *The Lighting Herd on Rainbow Mist
Island*, Preeti thought sadly.

Viren nodded. "But I wanted him to
stay forever!"

"Me too," Preeti said again gently. On impulse she bent and kissed his cheek.

"Yuck!" Viren scrubbed it away with his hand.

"Hey!" Preeti gave him a friendly nudge and he gave her a wobbly smile in return.

They walked toward the house hand in hand. Friends and relatives waved and

called to them. Laughter and singing floated out of the open door.

"Happy *Holi*! Happy *Holi*!"

The snow pony sparkled in the candlelight and seemed to turn toward Preeti and swish its tail. She felt herself smiling through her tears. *Take care, Comet. Thanks for being my friend. I hope you catch up with Destiny and take her home with you.*

About the
AUTHOR

Sue Bentley's books for children often include animals, fairies, and wildlife. She lives in Northampton, England, and enjoys reading, going to the movies, and watching the birds on the feeders outside her window. She loves horses, which she thinks are all completely magical. One of her favorite books is *Black Beauty*, which she must have read at least ten times. At school she was always getting told off for daydreaming, but she now knows that she was storing up ideas for when she became a writer. Sue has met and owned many animals, but the wild creatures in her life hold a special place in her heart.

Don't miss these Magic Ponies books!

Don't miss these Magic Kitten books!

Don't miss these Magic Puppy books!

Don't miss these Magic Bunny books!

#1 Chocolate Wishes

#2 Vacation Dreams

#3 A Splash of Magic

#4 Classroom Capers

#5 Dancing Days